YASMIN

The Astronaut

written by
SAADIA FARUQI

illustrated by
HATEM ALY

PICTURE WINDOW BOOKS
a capstone imprint

To Mariam for inspiring me, and Mubashir for helping me find the right words—S.F.

To my sister, Eman, and her amazing girls, Jana and Kenzi—H.A.

Yasmin is published by Picture Window Books, an imprint of Capstone.
1710 Roe Crest Drive
North Mankato, Minnesota 56003
capstonepub.com

Text copyright © 2024 by Saadia Faruqi.
Illustrations copyright © 2024 by Capstone.

Library of Congress Cataloging-in-Publication Data
Names: Faruqi, Saadia, author. | Aly, Hatem, illustrator. | Faruqi, Saadia. Yasmin.
Title: Yasmin the astronaut / written by Saadia Faruqi ; illustrated by Hatem Aly.
Description: North Mankato, Minnesota : Picture Window Books, an imprint of Capstone, 2024. | Series: Yasmin | Audience: Ages 5-8. | Audience: Grades K-1. | Summary: Yasmin is not sure she is cut out to be an astronaut, but a class trip to the space museum, and a tour of the mission control exhibit gives her another idea about how she could still be involved in the space program.
Identifiers: LCCN 2023021073 (print) | LCCN 2023021074 (ebook) | ISBN 9781666393910 (hardcover) | ISBN 9781484696224 (paperback) | ISBN 9781484696231 (pdf) | ISBN 9781484696248 (epub)
Subjects: LCSH: Muslim girls—Juvenile fiction. | Pakistani Americans—Juvenile fiction. | Astronauts—Juvenile fiction. | Science museums—Juvenile fiction. | CYAC: Pakistani Americans—Fiction. | Astronauts—Fiction. | Science museums—Fiction. | Museums—Fiction. | LCGFT: Picture books.
Classification: LCC PZ7.1.F373 Yap 2024 (print) | LCC PZ7.1.F373 (ebook) | DDC 813.6 [Fic]—dc23/eng/20230613
LC record available at https://lccn.loc.gov/2023021073
LC ebook record available at https://lccn.loc.gov/2023021074

Designer: Sarah Bennett

Design Elements: Shutterstock/LiukasArt

TABLE OF CONTENTS

CHAPTER ONE

A Visit Out of This World

"Welcome to the Space Center!" Yasmin read from a big sign.

She couldn't wait to learn everything about space on her class field trip.

In the lobby, the walls were painted with stars, planets, and even a black hole.

"Wow!" Yasmin whispered.

Mama was a chaperone.

"Please stay with your group,"

she told Yasmin, Emma, Ali,

Zack, and Mason.

"Isn't space beautiful?" said

a lady in uniform. She told them

her name was Ms. Simmons.

"Are you an astronaut?" Emma asked her.

Ms. Simmons smiled. "No, I work in mission control."

"That sounds boring," Ali whispered to Yasmin.

"I think I'd rather be an astronaut someday!" Yasmin whispered back.

"You can be anything you want, jaan," Mama whispered to Yasmin.

CHAPTER TWO

A Scary Ride

Ms. Simmons led them to a huge room. Inside was a shuttle as big as an airplane. Yasmin imagined going into space in it. That would be so much fun!

In the next room, they saw a
model of the Mars Rover. Then
they went to a play area that
looked like the solar system. It
had a sun and planets you could
climb on!

"My favorite planet is Saturn,"
Emma said.

Finally, the class came to a shuttle ride. "This will show you what it feels like to go into space!" Ms. Simmons told them.

Yasmin's group went first. Ms. Simmons strapped them in. The room went dark, and the doors closed.

"Welcome to the space shuttle ride!" a voice boomed.

Suddenly, Yasmin felt nervous.

She heard roaring engine
noises. Then her seat began to
rock back and forth. The ride was
loud and fast and scary. Yasmin
felt sick. She grabbed Mama's
hand and held tight.

When the ride was over,

Yasmin shuddered. "I didn't like

that," she said.

"I loved it!" Ali said. "That's

what astronauts get to do!"

Yasmin felt sad. "Then I don't think I can be an astronaut," she whispered. But no one heard her.

Three, Two, One, Liftoff!

The students ate lunch in the cafeteria.

"How do astronauts pack their lunch?" Ali asked.

"How?" Emma asked.

"In their launch boxes!" Ali said.

Emma, Mason, and Zack
laughed. But Yasmin didn't feel
like laughing. She didn't feel like
eating, either.

"Next we head to the control room!" Ms. Simmons announced. Yasmin and her group followed her to a room with lots of screens and computers.

MISSION CONTROL

"This is where we control the spacecraft," Ms. Simmons explained. "Mission control has a very important job. We make sure everything is working properly."

She pointed to a big, red
launch button. Then a voice
started to count down: "Ten . . .
nine . . . eight . . ."

"When we get to liftoff, I
want you to press the button,
Yasmin," Ms. Simmons said.

Yasmin nodded with excitement. This was an important job that didn't make her feel scared or sick.

"Three . . . two . . . one," the voice continued. "Liftoff!"

Yasmin pressed the button.

On the screen, a giant rocket launched into space.

Mama hugged her. "You did it, Yasmin!"

Ms. Simmons smiled. "Space travel takes a whole team. Without the team, astronauts couldn't do their jobs."

Yasmin smiled. Now she had a whole new future to imagine.

Think About It, Talk About It

* Yasmin wants to be an astronaut, until she realizes it might be too scary—and make her motion sick! Have you ever been disappointed because something you were looking forward to didn't work out the way you'd planned?

* Yasmin discovers that space travel requires a whole team. Which part of the team would you prefer to be on? The astronauts, the mission control workers, the rocket builders, or some other job?

* Yasmin and her friends got to learn a lot about space on their field trip. What are some things you know about space, the planets, the moon, or stars?

Write About It

* Have you ever been to a museum or science center? Draw a picture of what you saw there and include labels for your drawing.

* Make a list of the things you might want to be when you grow up. Then write the good things and not-so-good things you can think of for each one.

* Mama tells Yasmin that she can be anything she wants to be. Is there someone in your life who has given you encouragement like this? Maybe that person is you! Draw a picture of this special person.

Learn Urdu with Yasmin!

Yasmin's family speaks both English and Urdu. Urdu is a language from Pakistan. Maybe you already know some Urdu words!

baba (BAH-bah)—father

hijab (HEE-jahb)—scarf covering the hair

jaan (jahn)—life; a sweet nickname for a loved one

kameez (kuh-MEEZ)—long tunic or shirt

kitaab (keh-TAB)—book

lassi (LAH-see)—a yogurt drink

nana (NAH-nah)—grandfather on mother's side

nani (NAH-nee)—grandmother on mother's side

salaam (sah-LAHM)—hello

shukriya (shuh-KREE-yuh)—thank you

Rocket to Space!

SUPPLIES:

- empty paper towel tube or toilet paper roll
- washable paint and paintbrush
- large jar lid
- pencil
- colored cardstock
- scissors
- tape or glue
- red, orange, or yellow streamers

STEPS:

1. Paint the cardboard roll any color you like. Let dry. (This is the body of the rocket.)

2. Use the jar lid to trace a circle from the cardstock and cut it out.

3. Cut from one edge of the circle to the center point. Curve the paper circle into a pointy cone shape and tape or glue the cut sides together. Tape or glue the cone to the top of the rocket.

4. Tape or glue short streamers to the bottom of the rocket. Decorate the rocket however you'd like. You're ready for liftoff!

Saadia Faruqi is a Pakistani American writer, interfaith activist, and cultural sensitivity trainer featured in *O, The Oprah Magazine*. She also writes middle grade novels, such as *Yusuf Azeem Is Not a Hero*, and other books for children. Saadia is editor-in-chief of *Blue Minaret*, an online magazine of poetry, short stories, and art. Besides writing books, she also loves reading, binge-watching her favorite shows, and taking naps. She lives in Houston, Texas, with her family.

About the Illustrator

Hatem Aly is an Egyptian-born illustrator whose work has been featured in multiple publications worldwide. He currently lives in beautiful New Brunswick, Canada, with his wife, son, and more pets than people. When he is not dipping cookies in a cup of tea or staring at blank pieces of paper, he is usually drawing books. One of the books he illustrated is *The Inquisitor's Tale* by Adam Gidwitz, which won a Newbery Honor and other awards, despite Hatem's drawings of a farting dragon, a two-headed cat, and stinky cheese.

Join Yasmin on more adventures!

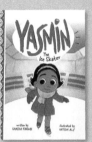

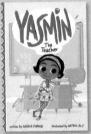

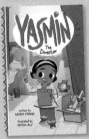